HER SCARS FROM WITHIN

WITHIN

"BEING ALONE WAS NEVER HARD BEFORE I MET YOU...."

RIDA HASSAN

Copyright © Rida Hassan
All Rights Reserved.

This book has been published with all efforts taken to make the material error-free after the consent of the author. However, the author and the publisher do not assume and hereby disclaim any liability to any party for any loss, damage, or disruption caused by errors or omissions, whether such errors or omissions result from negligence, accident, or any other cause.

While every effort has been made to avoid any mistake or omission, this publication is being sold on the condition and understanding that neither the author nor the publishers or printers would be liable in any manner to any person by reason of any mistake or omission in this publication or for any action taken or omitted to be taken or advice rendered or accepted on the basis of this work. For any defect in printing or binding the publishers will be liable only to replace the defective copy by another copy of this work then available.

Contents

Acknowledgements v

Preface vii

Prologue ix

1. A Girl Who Smiles 1

2. A Mysterious Boy 10

3. My Destiny 19

4. Praying For The Best 25

5. Another Missery 32

6. Forgiveness 44

7. The Real Horror 49

8. Pure Bliss 59

Acknowledgements

No creation of God is a solo effort. Neither this book, made with a lot of whack to make it reach to the hearts of people. It would not have been possible without the kind support and help of many individuals and organisations. I take this opportunity to thank them all.

I thank God for providing me with every possible means that I required for completing this small piece. I'm highly indebted to the Notion Publishing team for providing me a wide platform to showcase my work and also some other organisations who always gave a helping hand in the completion of this piece.

I would also like to present my gratitude to my high school teacher Mrs. Farzana zafar who always emcouraged me, made me participate in activites and always motivated me by her words like, " It's okay beta you can do it!". and mam it did it. Thankyou for always appriciating, supporting and being there for me.

Last of all but not the least, my sincere thanks to my parents, friends, and all those who have been instrumental in the successful completion of this book.

-RIDA HASSAN

Preface

The author chose a very dramatic, emotional and a twisting plot as the storyline talks about ones life incident full of joy and horror too. The author imagines herself in the character and wanted to explain ones pain and guilt who undergoes the situation.

The author's inspiration was her friend's life who went through the pain, emotions, love and horrors in her life which made her go silent completely. She had no one to talk to, even her friends hated her. So the author choose this topic to depict the student and teenage life of a girl going through all the life situations. To reveal this generation's thinking, emotions and guilt this topic was important.

It took about 3-4 years of thinking, researching, working and finding true and pure words to give this story a strong meaning. While hearing the story and thinking to frame it somewhere, it was also somewhere on my mind that I'll lack platform from where I can reach out to people and my story could remain hidden from people's sight. But I then strengthen myself realising that it will also be the same if I don't even start to write and may be then my story could bring me exposures and love from the audience reading my work.

Today I'm happy that I listened to myself and kept going with my heart and wrote this beautiful though heart-breaking story.

I proudly present to you our beautiful piece-" Her Scars From Within".

Prologue

This book is a work of fiction. The places, names and other matters related to the story are all fictional characters. Let me introduce you to the characters of this beautiful book.

- INAYAT - The main character of the story and the main asset as the whole story is about her and her experiences.
- ZAIN - Inayat's classmate and other main asset of the story who turned Inayat's life upside down.
- ROHAN and SARA - Inayat's most loving and helpful best friends.
- HIMANSHU, CHANDRIKA, RAHUL, AVIJIT, GULNAAZ, NEHA, KAYNATH - School friend group of Inayat.
- FARAZ - A sweet guy who comes with all the hidden twists and hell with him.
- Krish - The biggest mistake of Inayat's life which started the destruction of everything mattered to her.
- SHIZAAN - A sign of relief in her life who came with hopes, love and a spring of new life into her dead and haunting life.

These were the main charcters to be known beside these there are some more side characters such as JIYA, FIZA, INAYAT'S MOTHER and many more. You'll get a brief about them in the whole story.

" She wants
to be loved
with an
honest tongue,
devoted heart
and exclusive eyes".

CHAPTER ONE

A Girl Who Smiles

" No mummy please I don't want to go to a different city now, why can't we just stay here?" I asked my mother. "Beta, because your aunt is no more and there is no one to take care of your cousin brothers and our decision is final", my mother replied in a very subtle tone.

In a very small age, Inayat who lived in Kolkata had to leave her friends, her hometown, her school and everything she liked and have to move to a completely strange city Delhi because of her aunt's death. She was very sad and nervous too. Because she will be joining a new school and that will be a whole different environment for her.

"Mummy why can't we just call them to stay here with us?", I asked innocently with all the mixed feelings.

" Why don't you understand? I made everything clear before only. Don't disturb me I have many chores to do and you also go and pack your stuffs", my mother replied irritatively.

After two weeks of shifting, we finally got settled in Delhi and I aslo joined a new school –"Vasant Valley School, Delhi", where my cousin brothers were studying too. It was very hard for me to adjust myself in a complete unfamiliar environment. I also faced a lot of bullies, who made fun of my appearance, dressing sense and of everything I liked to do.

At first I was very scared of them and I didn't event had a friend to whom I can talk about things. I didn't wanted to tell all these to my mother as I knew my mother will only get worried about me rather I kept fighting alone. Sometimes I used to cry and sat alone in my room or remained quiet.

Slowly and steadily I understood that there is no problem in me but it is in them who bully me. I am perfect in my own way and I don't have to prove this to anyone and said to myself looking in the mirror " Afterall, a flower does not think of competing to the flower next to it. It just blooms and spreads it's own beautiful scent". This realisation was very important for me as I was loosing my self-confidence.

I slowly adjusted myself with a whole new mind set that now this is everything I have to live with.

Inayat had that 4'S when she joined school in Delhi at grade one which was Skinny, sensitive, shy and simple kind of girl. After few years now Inayat is in grade Ten and was not small shy girl anymore, she is now the monitor of her class. She was good in academics, extra curricular activities and now she is having a group of friends too. She is more than happy with her life and her cozy little family.

NO fear, NO anxiety, NO regrets and she also a teenager in a sophomore year.

Inayat as compared to her childhood is now very attractive, cute, bold and confident girl. She always makes everyone smile and laugh with her stupid humorous talks. She is very good at her academics (always a rank holder

), but she was in an intense fight with the subject mathematics. She hated mathematics like it's her enemy by birth. But still she always managed to somehow score good marks in that subject too.

"You heard about Rohan? Is he one of those new students who joined in mid session during the examinations?, Sara asked me. She was my very close friend or it'll be very inappropriate to call her just a friend because we were best friends more like sisters.

Me whose whole focus was at my studies replied while solving a mathematical equation," Umm no, I didn't heard of him". Sara, with a blushing smile kept talking "You know I have heard he is really very sweet and attractive and I came to know that our class is being allotted to him",she said with a excitement in her voice. I was still busy solving equations .

I replied teasingly " Tujhe itni khushi kyu hori hai? Tune homework kr liya kya? Kyuki sir to bilkul bhi sweet nai h and Rohan tujhe tuition toh dera nai hai".

Sara replied, "What is this yaar, tujhe har waqt padhai hi kyu karni hoti hai!", she then got up and went to the corridor. I saw her walking away making faces . I managed to give a small smile and then continued with solving my sums.

The other day was our mathematics exam and as usual I was very scared and anxiety hit me hard as it was my most hated subject. I got settled in my examination room and the exam started.

Few minutes later, I was deeply engrossed in solving the problems and was tapping my feet in anxiety. I had no clue that a new student is being introduced to the class. He was the same boy Sara was so excited about. Yes he was Rohan.

On being asked about the mathematics exam, he agreed to give the exam on the very first day of his school without any preparation like how can someone have this kinda confidence bruh and that too with mathematics... Ok cool!! Lets continue..

After the examination I was little tensed about how my exam went. I was then called by my class teacher for some work to the staff room as I was the monitor of my class. At recess time I noticed a new face roaming around in the classroom.

No other students besides her classmates were allowed to enter the their class while recess because there were many complains from students of their books being stolen.

I was already in a bad mood because of the exam and the presence of Rohan made me go MAD IN ANGER. I went to him straight away and asked him to leave the classroom immediately or I will complain about his behaviour to the class teacher and also gave him a threat of strict actions to be taken by the teacher.

Everyone tried to explain me that he was a new student but I didn't listened to anyone. Rohan got to know that i was unaware of the fact of him being a new student, so he thought of teasing me.

"Okay madam aap complain kar sakti ho but I'm not going anywhere, I love this classroom and your teacher loves me more than you", Rohan replied to me with a smirk.

I got triggered with his reply and was hating his smile which was trying to compete me. I didn't say anything and directly went to the staffroom and complained to the teacher about an unknown guy roaming inside our classroom and not listening to me when being asked to leave.

The teacher immediately came to the classroom with me and asked about the boy. I pointed her finger towards Rohan and said confidently "He is still roaming here mam!". Teacher smiled at me and told me, "Beta I think you were very engrossed in writing your exam. He is Rohan, one of the new comers and presently your new classmate. Please go have your lunch."

Teacher smiled and left me with embarrassment. Inside my head I screamed, " I literally hate this human!!", and I went to him and stood infront of him. On seeing me he again started to smile and said " Itna gussa na kro mujhpe I'm a good guy madam". I went to my seat making an hateful eye contact with Rohan while he was smiling at me.

Next day Rohan went to Sara. She saw him coming towards her and started to blush imagining every possible scenarios with him as she used to like him from the very first day.

I was in my classroom with my group- Himanshu, Avijit, Gulnaaz, Chandrika, Neha, Kaynath and Rahul.

Rohan introduced himself to Sara and she replied excitedly " Yaar tumhe introduction ki koi zaroorat nahi hai, I know everything about you and seriously you're so handsome!!". Rohan got a little awkward but he pushed the conversation forward as he wanted to ask about me " Inayat -the Great" and Sara was my closest friend .

So he continued, "Umm thank you but I wanted to ask your friend's name can you please tell me?".

Sara got confused and asked " Whose name? Almost everyone here is my friend, about whom do you want to know?". He smiled nervously and said "Yaar who tumhari friend hai na jo badi badi aankhon se gussa karti hai".

Sara burst into laughter by hearing such a cheesy description about Inayat and her reaction after getting to know this. Rohan got nervous and started to leave but Sara stopped him by shouting from behind, " Uss badi aankhon wali ka naam Inayat hai jao Rohan jee lo apni zindagi" and she started laughing.

Sara came to the classroom and our seat which was beside me as we were bench-mates too . She sat with me and started to tell me what Rohan did at the corridor. After hearing everything I started hating him more but Sara got something to tease us, which made Rohan happy but me aggressive.

Somewhere Rohan fell for Inayat's innocence and confident nature but didn't wanted her to know about this so early as he knew she hates him. So he thought of trying to make Inayat his friend.

Next day I was very nervous as I was going to get my mathematics exam marks and I didn't wanted to deal with Rohan on this day as I was already in a bad mood.

As I entered the classroom I directly went to my seat and my group came to me making me calm and positive about the marks. The teacher then arrived and I was sitting with my finger crossed .

Rohan was just observing her fear and didn't tease her for this moment.

To my surprise I scored very good marks. I was on seventh heaven and was happier than ever.

Then the teacher told that only one student scored maximum marks and I got excited to hear my name but my smile faded when I heard Rohan's name instead of mine , making me think of tolerating his disgusting smile again as he scored more than me.

But I was happy with my performance. I went home happily and excitedly showed my test paper to my mother and got praised by her. And got to have my favourite food for that whole day.

It was Sunday, I went out with my family.... enjoyed much and had dinner at my favourite restaurant.

The other day I didn't went to school as I wanted some rest. Next day at school, it was our P.T day so we went to play after recess. I enjoyed my day very much as my enemy was not present. My mood was very joyful and I was very happy after the results.

The other day, I noticed that Rohan was not present today also. This continued for about a month and I started to notice that everyone just kept staring at me with hate in their eyes except my friends from whom I could feel that they were hiding something .

Getting annoyed by their stare, I finally decided to ask my friends about the matter and what have I done to be a part of this hate. The other day with all the confidence I gathered, went to my friends and after some pep-talks I asked them curiously about Rohan being disappeared for a month now. She sarcastically said while laughing, " Dekha dar ke bhag gya mujhse" , hoping they would tell me something about him but they didn't .

With passing time I started to believe that I only did something because of which he is not attending school and that must be the reason why everyone is looking at me with hate.

Noticing my sadness my friends decided to tell me everything that has happened to Rohan which was going to be very intense for me but they could do nothing then to tell me the truth.

During recess time, instead of playing, laughing and sharing my lunch with my friends, I was sitting on my bench and kept my head down. They came to me and asked me if I am fine or not. After getting the surety of me being in a good mood, Sara sat beside me and started to narrate "Listen Inayat we can't see you like this blaming yourself without even knowing the whole story and we're sorry about lying the reason behind Rohan was not coming to school but now I think we should tell you everything that has happened".

Me in myself got a little scared , I felt a cold wave running through my body but I remained silent and listened patiently to what they were explaining to me. Himanshu continued after sara, " You know Inu? He really liked you and was just admiring everything you did even if you sued him away or shouted at him he wanted to be friends with you. But Kaynath (a member of our group) got to know all about this and she straight away went to the other section, spoke everything about Rohan to Zain".

Chandrika continued from where Himanshu left with a tensed tone " after knowing Rohan's feelings for you Zain became red out of anger and when you were not present the other day, during the dismissal time Zain and his friends stopped Rohan at the basketball court and he was all alone. And then...."

Chandrika stopped for a moment. I got restless and worried , " And then what Chandrika why did you stopped... woh thik toh hai na? Kya kiya Zain ne, tell me please!".

Chandika looked at Rahul and he said " Rohan got beaten up by Zain and his friends in a very tyrant way and he has been hospitalized since one month but doctors said that he will recover soon and can join school very soon".

I lost my control and went searching for Zain in rage. Zain was sitting under a tree at the football ground peacefully until I shouted and slapped him real hard. For a moment he didn't understood what really happened, after getting back into conscious he pleaded me to forgive him as he was just trying to protect me from the ridiculous intensions of Rohan and he had no personal grudges from him.

I was so furious that I just wanted to hit him and kept shouting " Mujhe Rohan se nai tmse bachne ki zarurat hai and you don't fucking need to tell me mujhe kiske saath rehna chaiye don't try to become my father when I don't even accept you as my friend nor as a human being JUST STAY AWAY FROM ME AND MY LIFE!".

And I took him to the principal's office and made him confront that he beated Rohan.

CHAPTER TWO

A MYSTERIOUS BOY

I started my schooling from Delhi, got admitted in grade one in which I met my classmates amongst which one was Zain.

Zain, he was handsome, fair, confident and fearless type of a boy. His thought process was like if something belongs to him it becomes his and he can't even tolerate someone else's eyes on it too.

I was unaware who Zain was until I came to grade seven and he once again became my classmate. This year was going to be a turning point in my teenage life which I didn't even had any idea about. I was a very focused student towards my studies and also used to enjoy with my friends during my free time.

Zain was all opposite of my nature and behaviour. He used to stare and attract girls and was in a habit of appriciation about everything he had. He didin't liked to study and he rather used to roam around with his friends. He was rarely spotted in the classroom and mostly outdoors. And these kind of boys were most hated by me. We didn't even knew each other and hadn't talked before.

Zain had a girlfriend and was always engaged in useless thing with his male and female friends.

One day he noticed me studing at the recess time when everyone else were chilling and roaming around. He to my seat and sat infront of me and said with a smirk, " AHEM!... Don't give this much stress to your pretty eyes they're too beautiful for this boring books, you can watch me instead..".

And I knew exactly how to respond to his ridiculous behaviour of his. I replied with a irritative smile "Grow up child, Iam not here for your sneaky childish flirts which makes you think those are your weapon I am a weapon in myself. Chose a wrong girl to dominate... Bad day for your ego...!". I took my books and went outside.

After hearing all the ill words from me he became very furious as this was the first time someone has challenged his ego and made fun of him infront of everyone.

After a month everyone got the news that Zain and his girlfriend got broken-up and everyones reaction was the same as everyone knew he could never be in love. And I was living my life as usual happy and focused.

When everything was running smooth, a shocking thing happend. During the recess time I was sitting under the tree at the ground and having my lunch and everyone else were playing and doing something of there own.

Suddenly Zain came and sat beside me. I was prepared as I knew how big of a flirt he was but to my surprise he talked to me very politely and appologised to me for the way the behaved that day. I was not ready to accept that he was same Zain who was such a ridiculous person a month ago.

He said to me in a very appologitic manner " Inayat I know i made you feel very awkward and I felt very guilty for the way I behaved please forgive me ." After listening to him i believed him and accepted his appology. He then extended a hand of friendship towards me and then me shooked hands.

He continued looking at my lunch " By the way can I have some It's looking so delicious and mujhe bahot bhuk lagi hai yaar!". I started laughing and then we both had lunch. The day went interesting and happy for me.

Two weeks later I got my first ever MOBILE PHONE...yesss.....that too in grade seven. I was so happy. everything was so perfect in my life it was just like a dream to me.

With Zain , our friendship built stronger and we used to talk alot and made alot of lame jokes. Then we got promoted to grade eight and again, same class we were happy that we were not seperated and I got to know Sara and we became best friends from then.

Everything was going just perfect but one day while having fun during the classes i hit him jokingly as he hitted Sara and I didn't knew what got into him and he got into his reflexes and slapped me infront of everyone. I was so numb i couldn't even feel what happened and why did he do that to me. I ran towards the washroom and started crying and I promised to myself that I'll never talk to him whatever happens.

While I was crying, Sara came to me and she started patting my shoulder making me calm but I was just not ready to accept the situation that just happened with me. Sara with her low voice said "It's okay Inayat please don't cry like this you're hurting yourself as well as me. It was my fault I shouldn't have hit him I'm so sorry.....please don't cry. He wants to explain himself please talk to him once".

I replied with a shaking tone "Just because it's explainable, dosen't mean it's excusable Sara. Nobody has the right to do this to me or any girl. From now on, he is just a stranger to me and i'll ignore his existance and kill him with my silence."

She nodded then I washed my face and we both went to the class. I didn't even looked at him and straight away went to my seat. He tried to talk to me but whenever he tried I ignored him or moved away from the classroom. This continued for two-three months and everyday a new face came to say sorry to me on his behalf but I ignored.

While all this continued to happen our first test took place, my test went awsome and as I was the monitor then too, I had to collect all the test papers from the students. So I got up to do that and I knew I was going to take Zain's paper too and this was the first time in months when he was going to be infront of me.

But I was confident and when i went to collect his paper he touched my hand while submitting......I looked at him and moved my hand away and went forward. It was his friend's turn to submit but instead he offered me a pen in which there was a letter instead of refil. I refused to take that and moved forward.

Then his friend shouted to Zain saying " Bhabhi nai maanri". After hearing that I was so triggered that i just wanted to slap him hard. Then I saw them giving a high-five to each other. I was so irritated, I went to Sara's seat and told her irritatively " You know what Sara, some people really deserve a High-Five in the face with a chair".

Sara started laughing and said " Mai to bolri hu tu baat krle ussey he has gone mad since you have started ignoring him. Pyaar hogya h usey tujhse meri jaan". I was so shocked hearing that from her " Shut up Sara and don't you dare think that i'll talk to him ever again faltu ki baatein mt kiya kar mere saath tu". Sara replied worringly " Acha madam cool down nai bolungi ab kbhi aisa ab khush!".

After few months, this day finally came IT'S MY BIRTHDAY!!......yeaahhh....my happiest day of the entire year. I was so happy, my parents kissed my forehead and gave me all the best wishes and left me to school with chocolates and promised me to spend the evening outside.

I went inside my school all dressed casually and excited for the day and guess what I saw my worst enemy and all my happy ,joyful mood went to the dustbin as he was staring at me. Just then Sara came running towards me and hugged me tightly, wished me and then she asked " Oyee what happened? Why are you in such a bad mood it's your birthday babe cheerup what happened?".

I replied pointing my finger at Zain " How can someone be happy? A spoiler is already present to spoil my mood".

Sara said sarcastically " Are yaar leave him and ignore his existance like you do everyday. Meri bestie ka birthday h yaar I'm the queen today" and we both started to laugh. Then we went to the class and everybody came wishing me.

Then the teacher wished me and everyone applauded and sang the birthday song for me. It was then time for dismissal. We prayed and left the school premises. Outside the campus, I went to my auto and sat alone as other students always came late.

While I was enjoying my own company I heard someone calling my name and to my surprise it was Zain's elder sister Amayra who was coming towards me. I was literally shocked and blank. I didn't knew why she was coming to me or what should I say to her.

After approaching She wished me and I thanked her politely. Then she took my hand and kept a small box and then she closed my fist.

I asked her about the box and her purpose. She answered, " I know you are feeling really awkward but you don't have to I'm just your friend and your well-wisher as well. I just came here to help my brother, dekho Inu he is very good human being and ussey galti ho gai jo har insaan se hoti hai and he is really guilty for what he has done to you please give him just one chanceand ye gift rakhlo usney bahot dil se diya hai tumhe".

After listening to her, I looked at her and then I looked back. He was standing behind me at some distance and was smiling at me. They moment flashed before my eyes when he slapped me and there was no regret on his face.

Anger took control of me and I crushed the box and threw it looking at him. Just then my driver uncle came with the other students and we left for home.

I made myself relax and said to myself that I should not spoil my mood due to some freaking bastard and I enjoyed the rest of the day with my family.

After a month it was his birthday, everyone was around him wishing, talking and laughing. I was minding my own buisness and the same thing happened the teacher came and asked us to stand and clap and sing the birthday song for him but I did the opposite of the instruction. I remained seated and looked out of the window .

I asked my bench mate to exchange the seats if Zain comes to distribute the chocolates from my side and my bench mate agreed. And as i thought he came from my side only and my bench mate betrayed me and he didn't got up to exchange the seats.

I was so dissappointed and Zain came and gave me five chcocolates instead of two saying " I know it's your favourite". After hearing that I gave all the chocolates to sara.

He saw me doing that and there was a frowning smile on his face but he said nothing and went away with his friends and left me relaxed for that day without disturbing me.

Few days went like that I was chilled as he was not chasing me anymore this is what my mind thought and made me relaxed but there is a saying that " Life dosen't goes according to what we think and predict but according to what has to happen, happens and we can't stop it from happening".

Our final exams were going to begin and the seats were going to be shuffled according to our roll-numbers. And I don't know what the teacher did to make roll-number 40 and 10 sit together. 40 was Zain and 10 was me, when she called our names together I was so shocked I didn't understood for a minute what was happening .

I turned and looked at Zain and he was happily smiling at me and the whole class were screaming like.......oooohhhoooo....good luck boy!!

It was the worst day for me as i have to share my seat with the worst person of my life who started loving me after hurting me as hell. I requested my teacher to change our seats but she refused and all my friends sat behind me.

I could do nothing but to accept the situation and adjust and keep ignoring him like I did before. We then settled down and gave our exams and as confident as I was with me he was blank as predicted he didn't studied a word and his whole focus was me. I completed my exam and sat facing my back towards him.

Sara sat behind me and she patted my shoulder saying " You're not like this Inu. He will fail his exams don't talk to him but atleast show him your paper please for me". I agreed and showed him my paper and after the exams i went to Sara's seat and sent her partner at my seat. I did this till the examinations got over.

After the examinations I went to Delhi for a road-trip with my family and enjoyed there much and had a great time with my family and create my best memories.

After coming back we went to school as our new session started and thank-god this time mine and zain's classes were different but he still didn't stop chasing. Everyday he came to my class window and from a distance kept staring at me. I used to ignore him as usual.

One day Sara went to him and talked to him that he should move on because I was having no intension of making him even my friend so relationship is a matter of concern. But he replied " I know that but I have some hopes left in that she'll someday come to my she is not heartless, she is just using her heart less and I love her even if she don't".

In this new session of grade nine I met my group of friends Kaynath, Himanshu, Chandrika and everyone else. Kaynath used to like Zain and was secretly jealous of me as Zain liked me. She always used to say bad words about me to Zain like I have boy-friends outside school, etc.

Zain used to ignore her and that made her more crazy. One day she went to Zain and made a plan. She said to him " If you make me your girlfriend then Inayat will get jealous and the love inside of her for you will become open as she loves you secretly".

Zain came into her talks as he wanted me. The next day when I came to my classroom everyone as cheering,

"oohoo congratulations Kaynath and Zain"

"you...both...look...sooo....cute...together...!!"

Opposite to their thoughts I became happy too and said to Kaynath " thankyou so much Kaynath finally he stopped chasing me and congratulations too". She was so very happy even if she knew their relation was fake.

Wherever I went I found them standing and doing romance which made me more happy and I started to ignore them more day by day. And then Zain came to know about how I congratulated Kaynath for their relationship and how she told him a fake story about me loving him secretly.

He was so in anger that he called Kaynath infront of everyone and broke-up with her exposing her ridiculous intentions about him and our friendship too. She came with an appology to me as I was disappointed of what things she madeup about me and that was the first betryal I had from a friend In my life. But I felt sorry for her too and forgave her.

The whole year passed by like this and now we became the seniors as we were now in grade ten.

CHAPTER THREE

MY DESTINY

"After the fight of me and Zain, Zain got the suspension for two months from the school principal. Rohan too joined back school but was little troubled to talk to me."

During the recess time I went to him and sat beside him and I asked " How are you? Are you feeling well now?". He nodded looking down. I continued " I'm so sorry Rohan this all happened because of me but I didn't knew this all will happen I'm really very sorry I didn't mean to hurt you like this ever in my life", and tears rolled down my cheeks.

He got anxious and worried and said " AREE AREE nai it was not your fault mai hi hero ban ne chala tha aur dekho kya hogya, please don't cry your eyes are so beautiful and tears don't suit you please". But I couldn't control my tears then he started making jokes to make me laugh.

"Tumhare ashique ne toh mujhe maar maar ke shole ka thakur bana diya hai now how will I give you my handkerchief to wipe your tears" and he started laughing and made me laugh too. And I laughed wiping my tears and hiting him jokingly. He shouted " OUCHHHH!!!..... madam mujhe aur damage mat kariye I'm already under consruction" and I laughed more.

He continued " Acha listen always smile like this you look cute when you smile and don't worry my feelings are mine I'm not going to force you on any note". I replied to him polietly " Hmmm... I know but I just want US to be good friends and nothing more as I don't have that kind of feelings for you and I don't want to give you fake hopes".

He nodded and said " Par maan gaye tumhe yaar kya badla liya tumne.. usey school se hi out krwa diya.. Good job Miss Inayat". And we both started laughing and I got one more best friend in my life.

Then I explained him the whole story behind Zain's involvement in my life. And his reaction was expected by me that OVER-ACTING one.

Everything was just running smoothly except Zain always keping an eye on me but I used to ignore him. With passing time Me and Rohan also became best of friends. Everyone was happy and life was like a pure bliss to us and we got lost into the sophomore years of enjoyment.

One day, two classmates who were just a casual friends of mine and their name was Jiya and Fiza, they came to my seat for a chit-chat. I knew they were gossip queens and as I was bored I got some company so I was lisening to them.

They were talking non-stop and suddenly took a pause, looked at me and said " Actually Inayat we were here because we wanted to talk to you about something very serious and I think you will listen to us once".

I nodded as I thought they were having some problem which they cannot share with anyone else so, I started listening to what they were saying.

Jiya started saying," Yaar we are here to talk about you and Zain. I know you hate him alot and you are right because the way he treated you he deserved this but Inayat ab bas yaar hogya bahot ab aur punish mat kar usey please!"

Fiza continued," Can't you see how much he loves you and everyday he comes with a hope that shayad aaj tu usey maaf kar degi but no you are in your own attitude and ego. YOU are hurting him way more than he desereves and we thought you are a good human being but no just look at you how cold hearted you have become that you can't even see his efforts of appology!"

And lastly the both stated a line which started haunting me day and night," You'll regret Inayat when you'll lose this love and everyone will hate you for this". And the went away leaving me feeling guilty, quiet and hating myself for my behaviour.

Sometimes life gives us twists for which we are not always prepared for and in that hurry to pretend the preparation we fail to win the race. And this is what exactly happened with me.

I started overthinking about what all I did but my heart was not able to point any mistake. I was all confused and messed and was not willing to talk to him neither my conscience nor my gut feeling was allowing me to do so.

But somewhwere in my mind that soul of mine said to me that my harsh behaviour has hurt someone so bad and how can I get happiness after knowing that I did something like this to a person who is actually appologetic and I'm not even bothered to listen to his appology once.

I said to myself even after all the deniels from my gut and conscience that I am not like him and I don't want to become him, So how can I treat him like he did.

This was the last conversation I did with myself and left for school. I saw Zain standing outside my window as always. I gathered all the confidence all called him. He was so shocked and happy at the same time that he thought he was hallucinating and asked his friend if he can hear me calling.

He came near the window and I said," I want to talk to you about something important If you are free you can come to the corridor during recess.

"How can I not be free I waited for this day for damn 3 years I'll surely come", he said happily and went to his classroom. There was some kind of a smile on my face which I didn't knew why it came and I was trying to hide it and be normal.

It was recess time and as expected he was standing there one period before the recess. With each step I was gathering all the courage I had in me and walked towards him.

I was standing infront of him and was searching for words, I didn't knew how to say or what to say. Before I could say something Zain held my hands in his and I got strattled. He calmed me and then I said, " I'm sorry Zain I know I went wrong all this time and I didn't even heard your appology once and I'm very guilty for that I don't know what to say more."

He continued softly, " I know but it's alright. I also did a ridiculous behaviour of slapping you and I'm really very sorry I totally deserved it but Inayat with passing time I felt your importance and existance in my life."

"When you were not talking to me everything seemed boring and lifeless, I didn't even felt like smiling. I came to school everyday just to look at you which brought some kind of happiness and peace within me. I missed you Inayat. Can we stay the same way we used to? " He said at once with A tear dropping from his eyes.

I nodded and then he smiled wipping his tears and lowering his gaze. And then he stated " I love you Inayat and I promise to keep my promise to always love and protect you. Will you come into my life once again but now not just as a friend but as a love of my life?"

I was just blank and many thoughts came to my mind but the words of Jiya and Fiza made me guilty and I accepted his proposal.

He was soo soo happy and was continuously thanking me but on the other side I was just blank as I had no such feelings for him and after accepting I started o realise I shouldn' t have said that.

In the strong wave of my emotions, guilt and overthinking I accepted him in blankness and now I was in guilty of a lie again.

We so often want love to work but we are fighting currents of our hearts that flow a different way.

I went to my class with all the heaviness in my heart and lost all the focus from my studies that day.

There was a emotion in my heart which was longing and humanity, It was not love but yes I was pretending to give my emotions a mask because I didn't wanted to hurt him more by saying the truth and I decided to keep up with him.

The next day the whole school was congratulating me and Zain and everyone was happy with my decision but I was not.

This whole couple thing was very new to me and I was just trying to sink in. With passing time I was getting attreacted towards him. His every small things started affecting me. His care, love and possessiveness started to become my habbit. His efforts started to become my liking.

I think I started to love him and the things which firstly I pretended were now real.

PRAYING FOR THE BEST

Yessss it's true I'm in love with Zain. I didn't wanted to but I couldn't help it. His love, care and fierce nature when anyone even puts a bad eye on me and his possessivness made me fall for him.

With time we became best friends in love. We used to share every little things with each other, made fun of each other , funny selfies , everyday I recieved his love letter with a flower at school and most importantly stayed with each other in our bad times.

It was all just like a dream come true to me such an understanding, cheerful, supportive and loving partner who was also adventurous just like me and old school too.

His parents were kind of abusive to him and mine were some times kind of pressurising. Time came when we only had us and again everything became normal. But this time it was not.

After school at evening when I was playing with my brother, I got a call from my friend that Zain was missing from his house and he didn't even came back from school. I got so worried as this was the first time he didn't tell me anything .

Everytime something like this happened I used to hug him and assured him of having me with him and said some calm words to relax him and everything got normal but this time I didn't even knew where he was.

I was very scared and started texting him knowing that he wouldn't reply but that's all I was able to do and nothing was in my hands. Somehow I knew, he would listen to me as no one could calm him ever except me because everyone is scared of his anger.

I started typing words to comfort him, making him realise even if nobody is there for him, I am and he has to come back for me and whatever came to my mind at that time I just kept typing them and thanks to God he replied.

"Don't worry I am fine now and I'm sorry I did this again to you. I'm going back home and will meet you tomorrow at school. Thankyou for being with me. I LOVE YOU."

After getting his reply I got back my breath and got little calm and went to school the next day. He hugged me and cried and I gave him all the time to become calm. He then became normal and held my hands and kissed them and said,

"Thankyou so much for being in my life. I don't know what have I done without you. I would not have even survived this phase of my life if you wouldn't have been with me. I can't explain how much I love you Inayat but I'll never break your trust ever I promise this." And we hugged again.

Everything was going very smoothly my academics,love life and everthing. I made Zain study with me and eventually his grades also started to get high. We were both very happy with each other.

But there is a saying - " All good things must come to an end". My life took a whole different turn and my whole state of mind got destroyed.

As the next day of school I saw Zain holding hands of my best friend Sara and Sara putting her head on his shoulder and Zain kissing her forehead.

I felt so numb. The land got removed beneath my feet and all I could feel was pain running through my nerves. I didn't wanted to believe what I saw . I was just wishing it to be a nightmare which will vanish as i'll open my eyes but it didn't. It was real.

My world was falling apart as both my best friend and my love gave me the biggest wound I couldn't even expect. The feeling of betrayal was giving me immense pain which was equal to feeling physical pain.

Tears rolled down my cheeks. I couldn't breath because of the heaviness in my chest, my face started to become pale and I couldn't help but fell down fainting.

I just saw Sara and Zain running towards me and then eveything blacked out. I opened my eyes and I found myself at the bed of hospital, seeing my mother crying and calling the doctor.

After being stable and letting the doctor leave my mother asked me about the incident and I lied to her of not knowing anything. She started scolding me for not eating and resting properly but I was just in a different zone of pain.

I was just getting illusions of them standing infront of me together. As I got discharged from the hospital I went to school as I knew I have misunderstood something and I found Zain with Sara again.

This time with a hope and heavy heart I went to them straight away. And I tried to hug Zain while they were quietly watching me. He pushed me away and said," What are you doing Inayat move away and don't touch me". I was so shocked.

Sara started laughing and said, " Poor girl isey abhi bhi lgra hai that you love her ".

I was just so shocked and hurt and quiet. I was just watching them while Zain said, " Tumhe kya laga mai aur tumse pyaar krunga have you lost it? Aree look at you and my standards. I was just trying to win my challenege as you insulted me in grade seven and I challenged my friends that I'll conquer you one day and see Inayat I won. I won why are you said baby? Meri khushi me mera saath nai dogi?"

"Chalo smile kro and clap for my victory. Best wishes hi dedo. Nai dena? chalo nevermind. Meri acting toh achi thi na? obviously thi yaar tabhi toh you fell for me, wait how can you not? you had to beacuse I wanted you to. Jaha pura school mere samne jhukta hai how could you have insulted me. Jhukna to tha baby."

And they started laughing and I fell on the floor on my knees all broken and shattered not ready to accept the reality .

Everybody laughed at me just my friend group was with me give me some hopes which I knew were fake and no hopes could make my pain less painful.

I stopped going to school for a week and my days days passed in vain . I wasn't eating properly , wasn't sleeping properly and was just crying and shutted people out.

But i had to somehow get out of this ain as it was getting a hold of me. I decided to get hold of y feelings and move on from everything that happened and forget about it just as a nightmare as I had no one but me to make myself feel okay.

"What is stronger than the human heart which shatters over and over and still lives" - I said to myself and left for school. I ignored everyone and focused on my studies and myself. Some laughed at me, some made fun of me but I knew what I went through and God is there to give a perfect reply when the time comes.

I eventually moved on. And I started becoming cold hearted and mean.

That's the tragedy of growing up. Knowing you'll run out of feelings for something new for the first time. The sad thing is you get so many of those moments, only a handful if you're lucky and then you spend the rest of your life turning them over in your head.

I think that's why you meant as much to me as you did, why I held on for so long. I didn't know it back then, but you were the last time I would ever feel anything new. Even the strongest of us breaks from time to time , we're just human at the end of the day.

One day I was passing by the main road for attending my tution classes and I saw Zain crossing the road and suddenly a truck came and hit him and he was there laying on the road all covered with blood. that love inside of me for him made me run towrds him and shout for help.

"Someone call the ambulance pleasee, he is bleeding too much, pleasee helppp!!". And they took him to the hospital.

I prayed for him ever since he got into the ICU. I begged to God for his life and good health. And by God's grace he was now out of the ICU and was in stage of recovery. When he got into his senses, Rohan went to the hospital to meet him.

He went into his room and asked about his health and his comfort. Then he said," Your love Sara is denying that she ever knew you and the girl whom you betrayed was crying and calling for help and till now she is praying for your life and good health. What have you done Zain? You broked her pure heart which started beating for you ever since she fell in love with you."

Zain said nothing and a drop of tear rolled down from his eyes. He said in a low tone of voice," I did all the evil to her and she is still praying for me. How came I did such non-sense with her. She hates me now , please Rohan I want to meet her , I want to say sorry to her and hug her. I don't know what got into me but I'll do whatever it takes to convience her . I love her man, I really do. Please help me bhai!".

Rohan agreed to help him and called me. I recieved the call and Rohan asked about me and how I was doing and then he stated that he has came to meet Zain. On hearing this I got worried and asked him , "Woh thik toh hai na? Has he got back into his consiousness ? Is he okay? say something Rohan Is he alright?"

Rohan answered, " Yes he is okay now. Doctors just want him to stay on bed-rest for a month and then he'll be fine to join school. and Inayat..." , he paused. I asked him what the matter was as he stopped.

He continued, " Zain wants to meet you ". I ran out of words and stumbled talking to him and said, " No, I can't meet him you know right ". And then Zain took the phone from Rohan and said, " Please Inayat for me please meet me once I beg you please". I agreed to meet him for 15 minutes on his request.

Next day after my tution I went to the hospital with Chandrika to meet him. We went into the cabin and

Chandrika greeted him and asked questions about his health while I remained quiet and he was looking at me. After few minutes Chandrika left the cabin leaving the two of us to talk.

Rohan said, " HI Inu". I anwered him back and he asked me to sit infront of him on the bed. I did what he asked and he kept his hands on mine and as he did that I started crying huging him. I couldn't control myself as I was so hurt and depressed.

I didn't wanted him to leave me neither did he. we remained like that for few minutes and the he started appologising foe what he did and now he is back to his senses and he realised how much he loves me.

I started to feel better in his arms and he was just patting my back and my head and kissed my forehead. And we got together once again. I was happy as he was with me.

The next day Sara came to me with tears in her eyes and held my hands and started crying and I felt she couldn't breathe because of crying so hard. I made her sit and gave her some water.

Then she started appologising for what she did and how she came into Zain's words and betrayed me. Seeing her so helpless and guilty I forgave her and hugged her.

Once again everything became settled and fell into it's place but soemthings things aren't the same as we think the are.

CHAPTER FIVE

ANOTHER MISSERY

Another wonderful day filled with peace, joy and love. I was chilling at my house after coming home and there was a ring on my phone. And to my surprise it was Zain.

"Hmmm toh...you can't even live an hour without me, itna pyaar mujhse han".

I said to him in a sarcastic tone after picking the call. But he remained silent. And in between that extreme silence I could hear his cold breaths which made me worried and anxious about something bad has happened.

"Hello.....Zain?....Can you hear me?....Are you okay?...Baby?"

I kept asking him repeatedly and after a few minutes he replied sobbingly,

"I'll....I'll have to leave you alone but I don't want to go away from you I want to see your face every day but now I can't, how will I live without seeing you!!"

After hearing this I got numb but I tried to calm him.

"Why are you saying all this, you will see me every day what happened You promised me you won't leave right then stop joking with me or else I'll not talk to you".

He made me feel like crazy those words were hitting very bad.

"My parents are sending me to Kolkata to study at a boarding school. Day after tomorrow is my flight. I don't know what to do".

Before I could say something he hung the call. I tried to call him many times but he didn't receive any of them.

At night I received a text from him.

"Meet me behind the campus after school. Don't worry. I love you."

I couldn't sleep the whole night I just wanted to meet him as soon as possible. Somehow I managed to survive the day at school and directly went where he called me.

I saw him standing and waiting for me. I ran to him and hugged him as tight as I could, he did the same.

I didn't wanted to go away from his arms, his fragrance which made me feel he is around me, his presence, the safety I felt with him and specially him, I was going to miss him a lot and that thought made me cry.

"Hey no, please don't, you are my strong girl right? Please don't cry. I'll not be able to go if you will cry please baby. I'll always be a call away and with you always in your heart. Please don't cry".

He said while patting my back and kissing my forehead, making me calm. He the lifted my face up and looked at my eyes.

"Joker lagri ho bilkul, you have made your nose red. Itna roogi toh flood aa jayega."

I hit him on his stomach and we both started laughing. We stood hugging and our forehead and nose touching each other. We were just looking at each other, hoping the time could stop and we could stay like this forever.

Slowly he pulled me closer to him grabbing my waist and touched my face moving some strands of hair behind my ear and my eyes were closed.

I was just feeling his touch and was submerging into the whole moment. He slowly came down to my neck, licked it and kissed it deeply and slowly. I was getting all the goose bumps and those tickles which I didn't wanted to stop.

I felt his lips coming closer to mine. It was going to be my first kiss and that too with whom I loved the most. I could feel his breath on my face as he was taller than me.

He then embraced my lips with his. I could feel his smooth lips caressing mine. He was kissing me passionately. I got butterflies in my stomach and that warm and fuzzy feeling making me go crazier for him.

Then I felt him hugging me which made me relaxed. He whispered into my ear-

"I really love you and I'm always with you. Always and forever".

Now I started feeling good but somewhere there was also a pain of not able to see or feel him every day. But I knew he is with me always and that thought made me calm and feel better.

And now it was time for me to go home. We hugged for a last time and then he dropped me home and went home for packing his stuff.

The next day I felt all alone in the school, my friends were there but Zain's presence was missing. After coming back from school I had my lunch and went to my bedroom for a nap.

The evening went waiting for Zain's call. Usually we used to talk through text because of my mother as she was strict but at this moment a call was necessary.

Finally after dinner I got his call. That was the first call in which both of us didn't say a word, instead we kept crying and at this point I felt how connected and attached I'm to Zain.

The night went like that and the next day every student went to the airport to bid him a goodbye. My mother also allowed me to go. We looked at each other and held hands and I said " I love you and I'll be waiting for you".

He nodded and went inside and then my normal life started as it was before Zain came into my life. I focused on my studies and took care of myself and at night I had long conversations with Zain.

Life was incomplete without Zain but as he was with me I was good.

But with passing time, Zain started giving me less time then he did before. I took that in a positive way and thought he must be busy with his studies.

Time passed and it was about two months since Zain left. It was our tenth grade as per the ritual we were going to have our first ever batch party. I was very excited about it and I told everything about it to Zain and asked him to come too.

But he refused as he was a new student in the mid of semester he had too much studies and assignments to complete. On hearing that my excitement went away and I said to him that I too don't want to go.

"Aree pagal ho? You were so excited for this. Please go and enjoy, ye din wapas nai milenge".

And he made me agree to attend the party. I showed him my dresses on video call and he chose a beautiful maroon gown for me and I just wished he could be with me.

I was getting ready and he called me asked me show my finally look to him. After looking at me he said, "Mashallah, teeka laga lo yaar nazar nai lagni chayye kisiki bhi. You're looking damn beautiful".

I started blushing and then we talked for few minutes and I left for the hotel.

As I arrived at the hotel, I found only some of my classmates sitting and taking pictures. After few minutes Sara arrived and I too got a company. We both started taking pictures and slowly everyone came and we got seated.

Suddenly I saw Zain entering the hall and coming towards me. I was soo soo shocked and I literally thought I was hallucinating until and unless he touched my hands which pulled me into the reality.

I was soo happy that I didn't care who is watching me I just got up and hugged him as strongly as I could.

"I missed you so much. Why didn't you tell me that you're coming duffer?"

I asked him by whispering in his ears while hugging him.

"Kyuki it was a surprise for you dumbo and by your smile I think you loved my surprise?"

He said to me while looking into my eyes.

"Ofcourse I loved and how can I not? I just wanted you to be here so badly. Thank you so much".

I said to him and hugged him again as I wanted to be close to him every moment.

He was looking so handsome in that full black tuxedo and now I knew why he chose this gown for me. It was going so well with his attire.

Then we took some amazing pictures of us and at that moment he told me that he has told his Mom about me and he also showed my picture too her.

I shockingly and shyly asked him about her reaction and he said that she was really happy after seeing me and she said,

"Mashallah, she is so pretty beta. I love your choice".

I was so shy that I didn't knew what to say or what to do, he held my hand and said "ye pictures Mom ko dikhaunga, you are looking way too pretty and he kissed my forehead".

Today we were with each other everytime. After all the games and cake cutting I started to feel hungry. Suddenly he looked at me and he understood without even telling.

He came to me and said " Chalo khana khate hai" and he held my hand and we went to the buffet. He didn't left my hand even when he was taking the plate or serving on it.

Everyone saw that and they started cheering. He looked at me and smiled and I smiled back at him.

He only took one plate and took me to the corner table and he started feeding me with his hand and he too ate from the same plate. I was so happy by his actions.

It was the first time ever that someone was doing all these lovely things for me. He even made me drink water by holding the glass and wiped my lips with the help of a tissue.

I couldn't find words to explain how happy and lucky I was feeling by his efforts.

Then he took me to the main sitting area and said

"Wait here I'm coming with your favourite ice-cream". I nodded and my phone rang it was my Mom just checking up on me.

I was talking to her when he came and sat next to me and asked me doing some weird actions that who is on the phone.

I smiled and I replied doing the same actions that it's my Mom don't say anything'

He said okay and quietly started to give me spoons of ice cream in my mouth.

As I kept the call, he noticed there was little ice cream on my lips. He wiped it with his thumb and licked it looking at the ice cream bowl without any reaction as it was just his reflex.

I was just looking at him and counting the amount of gestures he was doing for me and thanking God at the same time.

After having ice-cream we were just sitting holding hands and talking, our classmates started to play a game were we had to take out a chit from a bowl and we have to do whatever is written on it.

And Himanshu announced my name as it was my turn. So I went and took out a chit and it said,

"Do Ball dance with Zain". I was happy that I have to do the dare with him only and no one else.

But I forgot completely that he don't know how to dance so he started hesitating and denied to his friends when they were pushing him.

Suddenly one of his friends came to the stage and held my hand so strong that it began to pain and he said,

"Okay mat kart tu fir mai Kar lunga saath me". Seeing someone else holding my hand, he got possessive and he came running , jerked his hand from mine and agreed to dance.

He then and there learnt few steps from his friends and came back to the stage. The music started and lights became dim. The song was – " Meri ashiqui" from the movie ashiqui-2.

He came towards me looking into my eyes and kept his hand on my waist and joined another hand with mine. I kept my other hand on his chest and slowly we started to dance.

I was so happy, and after few romantic and close moves he got down on his knees and took out a ring.

It was the time I felt like was going to die out of happiness. Tears rolled down my cheeks and I hugged him tightly and said I love you to him.

He moved the ring into my ring finger while he was on his knees. Then he stood up and came close to me. He was so close to me that I could feel his nose touching mine and his slow breaths on my face.

He slowly kept his palms on my face and kissed me in front of everyone. I got lost in that moment. I didn't cared about people watching us. I could hear there claps, cheering and the sound of them capturing our beautiful moment.

He then looked into my eyes and said, "I love you too and I don't fear anyone".

I was so impressed by his gestures and fierce nature that my love increased with his every action.

The day went beautiful and then I left home and he went to the airport straight away because he couldn't afford to miss any classes as he could be in a huge loss.

At night me and Sara were talking about his sweet and manly behaviour and about how all the girls were jealous of me as they wanted to be treated like that.

Suddenly Sara said,

"Are you sure this time he isn't going to betray you, right?"

I replied taking a long breath and explained to her how we talked about this thing and took some steps which can sound childish but it just gives some sort of security as this is my first time in a long distance relationship.

He had my Instagram id and I had his. But I never opened his id ever as I believed him more than anything and he also knew that I never used open his id.

But from few days he was giving a lot of excuses for not giving me time and I never argued but somewhere I felt his behaviour was becoming weird as if few days before he was not even able to survive without talking to me and now I have become a burden to him.

I didn't wanted to have any of that thoughts about him but the way he was treating me I was automatically getting those weird thoughts.

And I couldn't help it and I opened his id and what I saw, I wished It to not be true and to be nothing but just my hallucination.

I saw a girl's chat in which he pretended that we had our breakup and we ended on bad terms. He actually made fake chats of mine to pretend the breakup.

The girl was from Kolkata itself and from his campus too. As I scrolled more I got to know he was cheating on me and he got physical with that girl.

After seeing all this I was completely broken as this was the third time he hurt me so bad and left me in tears. I was not even able to believe he did this to me again and this time in a worst way possible.

His call came and I didn't receive it. I blocked him from everywhere and changed my id's password, took some screenshots of the disgusting chat he had with the girl and then I turned my phone off.

I didn't even utter a word about him to anyone nor did I say anything to him. I just didn't want to let go the hold I got on my emotions. I did cried but at night when no one was there to hear me only my pillow used to hear my muffled cries.

Days passed, his friends came asking me why am I not talking to Zain and he is worried about me but I just kept ignoring them and didn't answer any of their questions.

It was the end of year we had our boards and surprisingly I did great and everyone was happy with me and I got promoted to grade eleven (Senior Year) and I chose Bio Science as my stream. But I was in a different zone I was in the starting stage of depression and nobody knew.

I used to cry at nights and doubt my loyalty, honesty, care and even my bare existence. I started believing that I am never enough and I can never be for anyone. I was so broke I didn't speak to anyone nor ate food properly.

I used to get irritated and angry very easily as everything became my trigger point. I was feeling just like a mess but always stayed normal in front of everyone.

I felt like a toy which he used whenever he wanted and then threw under the bus.

With passing time, I was preparing myself to move on when I found a stranger on IG. We started talking casually and as usual I remained sad. He asked me multiple times about my sadness but I used to change the topic or leave the conversation.

His name was Krish and he was from Mumbai, same of my age and grade. I used to relate much from him. He was a jolly, fun and full of entertainment kind of a person who made me smile with his foolish jokes.

I was getting stable and Krish was helping in that but one day when I went to school, at dismissal time I saw Zain standing in the same place where he gave me the memories which started to haunt me.

I tried to ignore him but then he joined his hands and called me to talk for once.

It was about 6 months, I didn't had a conversation with him and now he was standing in front of me with lowered gaze and I was looking at him straight.

"What? What do you want now? Wanna play more with me and my emotions? Wasn't all that enough?"

I said without taking a pause with a confident tone.

"You have misunderstood everything Inu, it's not what you think. I know you saw my chats but trust me it's not what you think. I can make you understand everything just listen to me please".

He said with a convincing tone trying to touch my shoulders. Taking a step behind I said,

"Don't you dare touch me and about which trust are you talking about han? The one which you broke twice. Okay then look at my eyes and say you didn't cheated on me".

Tears came to my eyes and I looked into his eyes but he lowered his gaze again.

"I was just attracted towards her nothing else baby I love you and only you please understand".

"OHH...wow Zain well played....slow claps for you. Remember the last time you wanted me to clap for you when you were with Sara, see I'm clapping now but this time for my victory. I won baby because my love was true."

I clapped while moving around him.

"I'm sorry Inu please forgive me. I did a huge mistake I shouldn't have done this to you I'm so sorry. Please come back please".

He started apologising holding my hand.

"You cannot leave and have me too; I cannot exist in two places at once! When you ask if we can still make it, remember what you did to me and I have moved on in my life. I have a boyfriend now who helped me cope all the shits you did in my life. So don't try to come into my life ever again".

I jerked his hands from mine and started to walk away.

I learnt one thing that day that – We shouldn't let someone's emotional inconsistency make us addicted to temporary highs and constant lows.

I went back home and took a hot shower and cried my eyes out and then went to my bedroom and I proposed Krish as I wanted Zain to stay away from me.

And to my surprise Krish said yes and claimed that he liked me too and was going to propose me in a day or two.

I didn't knew, if I was doing the right thing or not. I just didn't wanted Zain to be anywhere near me.

I thought that after hearing about Krish he will back off but I didn't knew this mistake of mine was going to turn my world upside down and destroy my life in every possible way.

I was in a state where I cannot make anyone understand. What is happening inside me. I cannot even explain it to myself.

CHAPTER SIX

FORGIVENESS

Another beautiful morning with chirping birds, scent of fresh flowers and those soothing rays of sun, sometimes confuses me that the creator created such beautiful and out-standing creations.

But on the other side, some creations of his are busy to break this beautiful saga and show how evil they can be to someone.

With this thought I got up from bed. It was Sunday today and I just wanted to stay home and live like I did before, normally, peacefully and free of every thoughts.

I hugged my mom as usual and sat on the kitchen counter and we talked, sang some songs and she cooked breakfast for me.

The start was really good, I felt home again......calm, relaxed and stable. Then I thought of watching some movie with mummy and she demanded to watch "Kabhi Khushi Kabhi Gum".

We enjoyed a lot while watching it but suddenly I got a flash of Zain and me in front of my eyes and I went numb for a moment.

I knew it wouldn't be easy to move on but I forgot it takes minute to have a crush on someone, an hour to like someone and a day to love someone but it takes a lifetime to forget someone.

I came to my room and went to my bed and started scrolling my phone to distract my mind. I noticed there was a text from Krish two hours ago.

"A beautiful good morning to my beautiful girl! What's the plan for today?"

I texted him back,

"Nothing special, just a movie date with mom and chilling at home. What about uh?"

We talked a lot and my mood became better because of him. He started to become more attracted towards me but my thoughts didn't allowed me to even think about Krish and if I'm doing right or wrong.

I completely forgot that I was in a relationship with him. And after few days I got to know some news about Krish and I was shocked.

He was in a relationship with 4-5 more girls and after coming into my life he ditched everyone because now he has true feelings for me. Then I got into my consciousness that everything is going to be a super mess.

And I should solve everything before it becomes a huge mess and goes out of control. I decided to talk to Krish about the misconception I had and I didn't knew what I was doing.

But in my case everything starts shattering even before I can try to repair. And the same happened a problem over a problem.

I was sitting on my swing at the balcony and suddenly my mom came with my phone. After all my weird moods and behaviour she thought of checking my phone.

And as I said I have a mind of genius, I didn't even bother to delete the chats of me and Zain. She read all the things about us and gave a kind reaction of breaking my phone in front of my eyes.

She then pulled me from the balcony to my room, pushing me towards the floor which made me fall and my head banged with the corner of my bed and started bleeding.

In that dizzy situation I answered every questions she asked and She threw her hands on me multiple times which I didn't felt on me as I was becoming unconscious because of bleeding.

She decided to tell everything to my father and the moment she called him I got fainted.

I opened my eyes to a complete different scenario. I saw my father standing at the door and there was a drip attached to my veins. My father wasn't speaking to me and my mom was missing.

I was feeling so very bad and guilty that my own parents were not talking to me but somehow I deserved it as I was the one responsible for this.

After few hours I was discharged from the hospital and my father drove me home. On our way home, there was a complete and weird silence and I was not able to look into his eyes as I was so ashamed .

We got home and my mother was still not talking to me. I went to my room and tears came running from my eyes.

After few hours my father and mother came to my room, I wiped my tears and sat quietly lowering my gaze.

Then they started scolding me a lot and in that condition also mom's hand didn't stop. Dad stopped her and then he warned me and then they both left my room leaving me in great pain, guilt, trauma and lonely.

They didn't talked to me for months and I remained quiet as well. I was attending my school and was not allowed to go anywhere else instead of school.

Recently I joined tuition for computer lessons as I was not able to understand the concepts. These were the two places where I found peace.

I as not even talking to Krish as I didn't had any phone to do so. But I needed to clear everthing as my life was taking way too many turns to damage me.

The next day when I went to my tuition, I borrowed a phone from a mate and texted Krish and told everything about Zain to him.

"This all happened and I was not in a conscious place and I did everything wrong. I'm very sorry Krish I don't have such feelings for you I don't even know why I proposed you but I'm literally very sorry and I can't talk to you anymore".

I said everything that came to my mind at that point but I said the truth.

He texted back angrily and in a revengeful manner,

"All this is a joke to you? Have you lost it Inayat Khan? Tune meri feelings ka Mazak udaya hai ab tu dekh ...*****".

And his text was followed by some highly disrespectful and ridiculous slangs. I blocked him and tried to didn't let any of it harm me as I am already tolerating a handful of abuse .

Everything was going good. Good in the sense my academics but nor with my parents neither with my life.

And the day came again. YESS MY BIRTHDAY!! but this time without any happiness or joy. I didn't even wanted to come out of my room and face people faking care for me for just one freaking day.

I was not even understanding the concept of them being happy on the day I was born as I myself regret of come to such a wonderful place and making it a negative hell for me and even for my parents.

But shockingly my parents came to my room, wished me and hugged me and I couldn't help but cry hugging them tightly as I was feeling so alone and lonely.

This got me the best present I could ever ask for- my parents. They started talking to me what else I could wish for.

The day brought me all the happiness that was taken away from me some months ago.

All I could say was that I am happy.

In all that happiness and peace I completely forgot that how can my life work out so well and how nothing is going wrong.

Before I could even think of anything bad, It started to happen. The real horror of my life started. Till now I have been seeing and reading about all this in news or posts but now it was going to happen with me.

CHAPTER SEVEN

THE REAL HORROR

It's the next day after my birthday and I am happy as my parents forgave me and were talking to me again. I knew I broke their trust and it's not going to be same but the thought of them talking to me and forgiving me was enough for me.

The day spent well and now the sun has gone down. Me and my mother were having coffee and some biscuits at the balcony on my favourite swing watching the beautiful sunset.

Suddenly her phone rang and it was an unknown number. Mom picked the call and gave it to me putting it on speaker saying it's one of my friend's call.

I thought of him being Himanshu but as I answered the call, the voice from the other side made me numb. It was Krish wishing me belated birthday.

I started over-thinking that how he got my mother's number and every possible scenario he is going to create.

But he kept laughing and saying weird things so I hung up on him.

My mother asked that who he was and about his strange behaviour.

"Aree nothing Mummy he was just a friend from my tuition, he is like this only one of a mental piece". I said with a stumbling voice and my mother started laughing.

I went to my room as it was my study time but all I could do was to get scared of thinking what he was going to do.

I took my brother's tablet and opened my IG id on it and I saw tones of texts from Krish.

Texts from him made me take a gulp of fear, horror and slander of me and my family's image in our society.

Zain got in touch with Krish and provoked his anger to the extent that he edited my decent pictures and pasted them and made them so vulgar that I couldn't help but locked the door and started crying and praying to God to help me.

They both started blackmailing me of posting those disgusting pictures of mine to adult porn sites and I was helpless.

Every day and night of mine became a dark hell for me. I tried to pretend a smile in front of my parents and friends as I had no one to whom I could share how I was dying every day.

I cried and cried and cried.... it made my eyes burn and some drops of blood also came. I felt suffocation, disgust of my own body, I also had panic and anxiety attacks as I was going through that phase all alone.

Their faces started to haunt me. I became scared more and more every day. I became depressed, lonely, alone, hopeless and I just wanted to die.

They wanted me to send them nudes of mine every day or else they were going to post what they created for me.

Every night I came to my room and looked myself at my mirror. I looked so helpless and scared. I removed my clothes one by one looking towards the sky asking God to give me death.

I was tired of being their slave. I was angry, I was in deep pain, I was scared and the one day I decided to end this horror and I attempted suicide.

I took the knife from the kitchen, came to my room and once again I looked at myself in the mirror,

"I'm so sorry Mom and Dad but I have no other option than to see you in pain. I can see you tolerating this pain but I can't see you tolerating the pain which the society will give you. Your daughter loved you a lot but she failed to stand strong before those two animals. I'm sorry please forgive me".

I said to myself crying and then I kept the knife on my veins and closed my eyes and everything became numb.

I could feel all the pain leaving my body slowly and I smiled and then darkness took over me.

But who can save you from the sufferings that are written for you. No matter how much you try to run from your fate, you can never win.

My eyes opened slowly, I was in a hospital. I could see my parents praying, crying and hoping I could get back into consciousness.

I also saw a very familiar face. He was a very old friend of mine, Faraz. We were society friends when I used to stay in Kolkata. I got confused that what was he doing here after so many years.

Just then when I was deeply engrossed thinking about his presence, my parents and Faraz came running to me.

Mom and Dad they both hugged me and on getting that warmth my heart melted and tears came running from my eyes.

They asked me if the wound is paining or not. I didn't know how to tell them about my real wound and how much I'm tolerating the pain, the horror and the fear inside of me.

My parents thought that I took this step because of my studies. So they came to my cabin at night and talked to me very politely about the matter and loved me. Then Mom fed me and told me not to take stress or worry about my studies and then they left.

The nurse came and gave me an injection which pulled me into deep sleep. That was the first night I slept so peacefully.

The next day after having my breakfast I was taking rest and just then I saw Faraz again. This time he didn't disappear and instead he came into my cabin.

"Hey! How are you feeling now?"

He asked softly.

"Much better from yesterday. How come you're here?"

I asked him in a low tone as I felt pain in my hand.

"I got shifted here yesterday only and thought to give you a surprise but when I came to your house it was locked. So I inquired and got to know that uncle got sick. So, you all came to this hospital but when I came here I saw you, aunty and uncle told me everything that happened".

"When did you become this coward that just because of studies you did this to yourself? Where is that strong Inayat that I used to play with, who used to protect me from everyone?"

He asked me surprisingly and in a soft tone wanting to encourage me.

"Is there anything else? I don't think you can ever do something like this to yourself just because of studies. No! I cannot agree to this. If there is something, you can share with me without any hesitation. I'll try my best to help you Inayat".

On hearing his words I began to cry, and I told him everything that was going on.

"You were going through all this and didn't even bother to remember me".

He said while lowering his gaze and his tone said that he was feeling sorry for me.

"I was nor conscious neither stable with my state of mind that's why and I was scared too that even if I tell someone how they will react".

I replied while wiping my tears in a painful voice.

We talked for hours and then in the evening I got discharged. I was not attending my school too as they texted everyone in the campus how characterless I'm.

I kept attending my tuitions where Faraz also joined and made me feel better about things and told me to deactivate my id on IG and not to keep any contacts with them.

I did what he said and it really helped me there was a kind of fear still residing in me.

After few months it was my final exams and I went school. To my expectations no one was talking to me except Sara.

Somehow I gave all my exams and the result came and my scores where average but my parents encouraged me as I was in the second stage of depression.

Faraz and I continued with our tuitions and we were both promoted to grade twelve (our last year at our schools).

One day while doing our work at the tuition Faraz asked me to come to his house after tuition as it was his birthday and I apologised for not remembering his birthday but I denied on coming to his house.

He kept insisting then Sara came and said, "Chal na yaar tu itne dino se kahi gai bhi nai and tera mind bhi fresh ho jayega. Don't worry aunty se mai baat kr lungi".

Then we all went to his place and Faraz introduced me to all his friends. Then it got late and almost everyone started to leave. So I went to him and said,

"Faraz, thank you for inviting us but now it's getting late and mom must be worried now. I think I should leave now".

I said to him very politely and with a smiling face.

Just then I heard someone from behind of me saying in a laughing tone "Itni jaldi kya hai humse nai milogi ?"

My body started shaking from head to toe as I knew those two voices very well.

My fear was going to change into reality in a moment or two but I got shaken that Sara was involved in everything from the start and betrayed me once again.

Faraz was just standing and seeing everything. I saw into his eyes, he wanted to help me but there was something that was stopping him. He said sorry to me while I got pulled by my hair and got thrown on the floor.

Yes they were Zain and Krish .

Zain came closer to me and I tried to move back using my hands and legs but he came closer to me and pulled my hair and held my cheek with his other hand pressing it very badly.

"What did you say Tu jeeti han? Jeet toh ab tu dekhegi bahot zubaan chalti hai teri"

He said and pressed my cheeks more and then slapped me. Krish came from behind and pulled my hair again and threw me to the other corner of the house.

He then started twisting my hand and I screamed in pain and begged them to leave me but they didn't hear any of my cries.

They were beating me badly and screaming disgusting words near my ear but I looked at Sara and she was enjoying everything. I begged her to stop them but she spat on my face and said,

"You deserve this entire thing bitch. Bahot attention milti thi na tujhe school me and koi mujhe kuch nai smjhta tha ab bhugat"

They started removing my clothes and I started scream more and tried to stop them but they gave me more pain and I looked at Faraz but he was standing expressionless.

At first I thought he was sorry but he wasn't he was just playing his victim card.

I felt an immense pain which felt like all my bones broke at once. They tried molesting me. I was feeling so helpless that I was just looking up and taking names of God and begging them to leave me but they started beating me again.

I was so in pain, I now started to pray that they kill me as I had no reason to live anymore.

After sometime they got up, got dressed, laughed at me and went away. Sara and Faraz also disappeared.

I got up crying, not able to walk properly, got dressed and somehow reached home. I was just a dead human whose body was alive.

As I reached home I saw my parents note as they were at some function. So, I straight away went to my room, sat on the floor and started to pray. I cried my heart out to God.

Then I went to the bathroom to take a hot shower and I saw my body. It was all covered with cuts and bruises.

After that day they used me like that many times as I didn't had any courage left in me to even ask for help or to take a stand for myself.

And all I did was to come home, cry, take a shower and hate myself and feel disgust about my body and soul.

I was at a point where I lost all my hopes and started believing that may be I was made for this pain or maybe I deserve this all.

But a time came when I was just full and I wanted to end everything.

I got a call from Sara again on my mom's phone , it was there way to call me at Faraz's place. As soon as I heard her order I shouted at her with all the strength I had in me

"NO.....NO...NO...I WILL NOT FOLLOW YOUR ORDERS ANYMORE....YOU BLOODY MOLESTERS!!"

And I hung the phone. My mother came running on hearing my voice and found me shattered and crying on the floor.

She got worried and tried to ask me about what was happening. I told her everything and after hearing my pain she hugged me and started crying. We remained like that for some moment.

Some days passed and again a call came from an unknown number. It was them and I got scared but my mom hugged me and made me calm and she picked up the call.

And to my surprise they all started apologising to my Mom one by one and my mother shouted at them a lot she cried while shouting to them and she kept screaming at them for hours.

Then she threatened her of sending them behind the bars if they ever try to harass me or try to get in contact or found near me.

Then she hung up on them and hugged me. I cried a lot and I felt a relief from my shoulders.

She then made me calm and gave me a glass of water. Then she started discussing with me about sending them behind the bars but I stopped her, thinking about how the society will make a hell for my parents.

I also thought about how my father's heart will wrench out in pain after hearing what his daughter was going through and what will happen to the pride with which he stated my name in crowd of me being his daughter.

My mother understood what I was trying to convey, so she agreed. But she called each and everyone's parent and told them what their children did to me and they came to my house to apologise to me.

I also heard that Krish's parents threw his stuffs out of the house and Sara was not allowed to attend school anymore.

And Zain he was already dead for me. Days passed but that horror didn't left me. I was in the last stage of depression.

My mother started to take me for counselling and it helped me a lot but still depression gives a great depth of memory depression in our mind, soul and heart.

I passed out from School with good grades and I created a wall around me. I didn't talked to anyone much.

I started to burn, freeze; I am never warm.

I am rigid now; I forgot softness because it did not serve me and the tired sunsets and the tired people—It takes a lifetime to die and no time at all.

Every day I try to take a step up not even realising I'm walking backwards. Every day it gets a bit worse, a bit more down and I don't know if I'll ever get to the bottom.

I don't know where the bottom is, thought I had reached it many times already but there are not many pieces left on my heart to break.

There is not any hope left that could be taken away. I don't know where the next step leads to, how could I ever endure more of this.

CHAPTER EIGHT

PURE BLISS

Today it's been two years past the disgusting incident happened with me. I'm preparing for my entrance exams now and have become mature with time.

This new Inayat who faced things in such a small age, is now responsible enough about all the works.

I used to stay quiet a lot and rarely smiled. I have few friends now which I don't trust with my whole heart till now as I have had enough of betrayals and there was no such place left for more .

Now I used to stay quiet instead of arguing and let people think they are right in everything matters even if they weren't.

I was living my life normally and dealing with my depression too. I still had some panic and anxiety attacks but I never let anyone know.

I used to deal with all my problems alone and became kind of rude to strangers and some time to my loved ones too.

As I created a wall around myself because I was not able to trust anyone anymore and the thought also remained the same that I don't deserve those fancy words like love, care, etc.

I didn't had any expectations from anyone I knew that:

In this crowd full of false, I have built up my walls. No windows and no doors. For those who are real, the wall simply falls.

Like this I was going with my life When suddenly I received a text on my IG-

"Assalamu alaikum"

It was a greeting in Arabic language (peace to you, which was from a stranger.

As I said I didn't talked to strangers anymore but as a human being I needed to reply his greeting with " Walekum assalam" as per Islam.

I asked him if he knows me but he said

"I know you but you don't, I'm a friend of your common friend".

I felt weird about the way he talked as he was trying to hide his identity.

"Which friend and why did you texted me"

I asked him confusingly to which he again gave an weird answer.

"I can't tell that as I have promised her to keep her identity safe and can you tell me where do you live?"

As everything became my trigger point because of depression, I became irritated and angry due to his strange behaviour.

I told him that if he doesn't tell me how he is I'm going to simply block him.

As I thought of him being Zain or Krish I was angry much.

But he made me calm with some of his words and told me about him.

"I'm Shizaan Khan and I live in Delhi only. I don't want to scare you but I only want to have a friendship with you and I have no bad intensions for you".

I was still angry and replied,

"Aree how can I have a friendship with you I don't even know who you are and why are you here and you're hiding you're identity too. Why are you not showing me your picture?"

He replied,

"I want to know you and tell you about me slowly as I told before I have no bad intentions for you but for this to happen you also have to give a hand for friendship"

I Listened to him and thought about this for some time then I agreed.

We started talking and he always left the conversation leaving me in curiosity to know who is he.

But slowly he revealed his identity. He told me about his job, his family and where they lived which made me a little comfortable.

I didn't knew when I started sharing everything with him and till know I haven't seen him or knew where he got my id from.

Other than that I knew everything about him and except my secrets, he knew everything about me.

With time we became very good friends and I started feeling something for him. It was feeling just like a movie.

One day he told me that now our friendship has become strong so he is going to send me a picture of his.

On hearing this I got a little nervous and curios at the same time.

He started teasing me by sending half of his picture and I became angry then he sent his full picture.

When I saw him there was a kind of smile on my face. He had a trimmed beard and a nice personality and I felt I was attracted towards him.

We then started joking and talking more. I started to notice some lines that he used and after using them he hesitated which made me believe that he likes me.

Days passed and I waited that when he will accept his feelings for me but as expected he didn't as he was way too shy .

The other day we were talking and I said about something, in which he replied,

"Aapkoye pta h ki aap mere liye kitni zaruri ho"

And as usual he started hesitating and tried to change the topic but this time I didn't let him and asked him continuously to say the truth.

He got trapped and now he had no other option but to tell the truth.

he stared from the beginning and said,

" I went for some work near your area, and was going to leave when a pairs of beautiful eyes and strong aura caught my attention. You were passing by with your lowered gaze and when I saw you I felt like the time have stopped and all I could feel was butterflies in my stomach"

"I was very confused what to do. I thought of following you or to stop you there only but then I thought of getting slapped by you."

"I wanted to tell someone that this has happened to me but I was unable to do so. Every day I came in that area after my job hoping to get a glimpse of you for once but I didn't see you."

I was hearing everything he has to say without disturbing him and there was a blush on my cheeks. He continued with his narrative,

"I searched for you in that whole area but failed to find you. Then I contacted my friend, who knew everyone in that area and I gave a description about you but he made fun of me that I don't even know your name and may be I'll not be able to find you".

"But I didn't become hopeless; I continued the search for you. And started praying to God that if I ever get to see her please let her be in my fate forever".

"After a long wait of a month I saw you again in a family function and my eyes were not ready to miss a single look of you."

"Those similar big and beautiful eyes but I was not having the confidence to come and confront my feelings for you"

"Then a lot of crazy searching I finally found your id from my friend's friend who was your senior in school but you were not familiar with her and luckily she knew about you".

"This was a very big thing for me but I didn't know how to approach. So, I started planning in a dairy and as I didn't knew your name, I named it as 'MISSION NAZAR'."

"I wrote every possibilities of how you could react or block me and then started the conversation with you. As per my expectations, difficulties came but I remained honest and told you the truth slowly so that the conversation could remain constant hoping you will accept my friendship."

"And thankfully you did and know Inayat I want you to know that I really love you and respect you. I never had any bad intensions for you, just my pure feelings and I'll be the happiest if you accept my love and agree to come into my life and make it more beautiful. Will you?"

I was so happy, excited and was blushing too. I was feeling this kind of happiness after years and didn't wanted to let go of it.

But the fear took me again. What if he'll do the same? What if he is also one of their friends?

I decided to tell him everything before giving any answer to him as I didn't wanted to hurt him nor give any third person the opportunity to break our bond.

"Before I give the answer, I want to tell you about my deepest and darkest secret. I don't know after knowing it what your reaction will be but it's important for you to know it".

And I told him whatever happened with me and how I have become aster everything.

After hearing to whatever I had to say, I reacted in a very calm way and was feeling sorry for me.

He reacted very positively and assured me of having him by my side from now and promised me to protect me from everyone.

I was so happy to hear all that from him and then he asked,

"So, will you now?"

"Yes..obviously...I will!!"

I said with tears of happiness as I finally found a true companion who loved me even knowing my worst and still made me feel the best.

After all the bad phases, getting him in my life was worth everything. He helped me overcome my depression and took the best out of me. And I'll be grateful to him all my life.

But it's a nature of a wound, it leaves behind a scar. And I had a lot of scars from my past. The scars don't hurt anymore, but I can't forget the way it used to.

If she dosen't say what she wants, If she dosen't say how long she waits,

It is the flaws of her way the surrender words, Through her calmness,

Flowing from the hidden volcanoes. The feeling she kept for you,

Remains from the pending ages, She ever wished to live for you.

Don't ask the wounded bird why she left,

If the branches were fake, The dreams wouldn't stay.

Don't challenge the revenge of the waves when it erupts

the skills of her stormy silence.

If the ocean dosen't say, Don't blame the depth if her soul didn't...